Nate the Great
and The
PHONY CLUE

Nate the Great
and The

PHONY CLUE

by Marjorie Weinman Sharmat

illustrations by Marc Simont

A Yearling Book

Published by Yearling, an imprint of Random House Children's Books
a division of Random House, Inc., New York

Visit us on the Web! www.randomhouse.com/kids

Educators and librarians, for a variety of teaching tools, visit us at
www.randomhouse.com/teachers

ISBN: 978-0-440-46300-9

Reprinted by arrangement with Coward, McCann & Geoghegan, Inc.
Printed in the United States of America
May 2007
64 63 62 61 60 59 58 57 56

For 133 Dartmouth Street

, Nate the Great,

am a great detective.

I have just solved a big case.

It did not look

like a big case when

it started this morning.

My dog, Sludge, and I
were running
around the block
for exercise.
We ran past Annie
and her dog, Fang.
We ran past Rosamond
and three of her cats.

We ran past Finley
and his friend Pip.
We ran home.
I saw a piece of paper
on my doorstep.
I picked it up.
It was thin paper.
VITA was printed in ink on it.
The paper was torn off
around VITA.

What did it mean?

I got my dictionary.

I looked up "vita."

I found that "vita" could be

the start of a word.

"Vita" could be the start of
"vitamin" A, B_1, B_2, B_6, B_{12},
C, D, E, G, H, K, or P.
Or "vita" could be the middle
or end of a word.

It could even be

part of a long message.

The mystery got bigger

as I thought about it.

I, Nate the Great, knew

there was a missing piece or pieces

of the paper.

Who or what had torn them?

I let Sludge

sniff the piece of paper.

"We will look for the pieces,"

I said.

I, Nate the Great, thought.

Who or what tears paper?

Of course! Rosamond's cats.

Four cats. Sixteen claws.

Sixteen claws could tear
a lot.
I wrote a note to my mother.
Then I tore it into pieces.
Then I fitted the pieces
back together.

I put a pancake in my pocket.
Then Sludge and I went
to Rosamond's house.
Rosamond was outside

with three of her cats.

Rosamond looked strange.

But she always looks strange.

"Hello," I said. "Did you

leave a note on my doorstep

this morning?

Did your cats tear it?"

"No," Rosamond said. "I did not

leave a note on your doorstep."

I looked at her cats.

They looked strange, too.

"My cats have been with me
all morning," Rosamond said.
"Except Big Hex. Big Hex
spent the morning
in his favorite tree."
"Big Hex tears paper," I said.
"Yes," Rosamond said.
"Big Hex tears, rips,
scratches, shreds, cuts,
slits, and slashes."
"I see," I said.
"Did Big Hex tear,
rip, scratch, shred, cut,
slit, or slash
a piece of paper today?"
"Ask him," Rosamond said.

I looked up.
I saw Big Hex
sitting on a branch
of the tree.
I, Nate the Great,
was in luck.
I saw a piece of paper
stuck on a twig
close to Big Hex.
Too close.

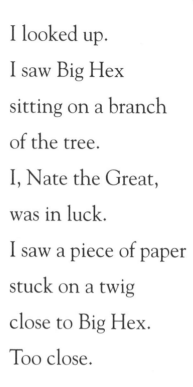

I reached into my pocket

and pulled out the pancake.

I threw it on the ground.

Big Hex jumped down and started

to eat the pancake.

I reached up and grabbed

the piece of paper.

Now I had two pieces.

I put them together.

"They fit!" I said.

"It *is* a message. Look.

Now the paper says

INVITATION

COME TO MY HOUSE AT THREE.

'Vita' was part of 'invitation.'"

"You solved the case,"
Rosamond said.

"No," I said. "There is still a
missing piece with a name on it."

"What name?" Rosamond asked.

"The name of the person who
wrote the invitation," I said.

"I, Nate the Great,
will find the missing piece.
I will find it before three."

I started to leave.

"Wait," Rosamond said.

"Big Hex wants to thank you
for the pancake."
"How does Big Hex thank?"
I asked.
"With a kiss," Rosamond said.
I, Nate the Great, did not
want to be kissed by anyone
who tears, rips, scratches,
shreds, cuts,
slits, and slashes.
"No thanks for the thanks,"
I said.
Sludge and I ran home.
It was time for lunch.
I made some pancakes.
I gave Sludge a bone.

We ate and thought.

Where was the missing piece

with the name on it?

I, Nate the Great, had to know

by three o'clock.

Sludge and I started out again.

I saw Annie and her dog, Fang,

coming down the street.

They were with Finley and Pip.

Pip does not say much.

Finley says too much.

"I, Nate the Great, am looking

for a piece of paper

with a name on it," I said.

"Why are you great?" Finley asked.

"I solve cases," I said.

"I find and I find out."

"Why don't you find the piece
of paper?" Finley asked.

"Nate the Great will find it,"
Annie said.

"Ha!" Finley said.

"Maybe he's great;
maybe he's not."

Pip said nothing.

Finley and Pip walked away.

Sludge turned and followed them.

I turned and followed Sludge.

Annie and Fang turned
and followed me.

I saw Finley drop a piece

of paper into the sewer
and walk away.
I looked into the sewer.
I did not like
the way it looked.

But the paper was there.
It could be the missing piece.
How could I get the paper out?
I, Nate the Great, needed
something long and sharp.
I saw something long and sharp
beside me.
Fang's teeth.

Then I had another idea.
I looked down
at the paper again.
It looked blank.
"The print must be on the side
that is facing down," I said.
"We must wait."

"Wait for what?" Annie asked.

"Wait for the water in the sewer
to make the paper very wet.
The invitation is printed
in ink on thin paper.
When paper is thin and
the printing on it is dark,
water can make the printing
show on the other side.
Then we can read the name."

"But won't the printing
look backward?" Annie asked.

"Yes, but nothing is perfect.
I, Nate the Great, say that
nothing is perfect."

The paper was getting

wetter and wetter.

I saw some printing on it.

I saw . . .

"Phony clue!" I said.

I, Nate the Great, was mad.

I had never had

a phony clue before.

I did not know what to do.

I could not find the missing piece.
I looked at the pieces in my hand.
I, Nate the Great, thought.
Then I said, "I am looking
at what I have.
Perhaps I should look
at what I do not have."
"How can you do that,"
Annie asked,
"when you do not have it?"
"Look!" I said. "When I put
the two pieces together,
the empty space that is left
is shaped like a boat.

So the missing piece
is shaped like a boat.
I, Nate the Great, will
look for a paper boat."
"What if you can't find it
before three o'clock?"
Annie asked.
"Then I am sunk," I said.
Sludge and I walked and thought.

I, Nate the Great,
had seen a boat today.
But where?
It was not
on the Atlantic Ocean.
It was not
on the Pacific Ocean.
It was on a paper ocean.
Sludge and I ran
to the paper ocean.
The paper boat was there.
I fitted my pieces
of the invitation
around it.

Aha! They fit. The paper boat
was the missing piece.
The paper boat was . . . blank.
It did not tell me anything.
Or did it?
Now I knew that someone
wrote an invitation to me
and did *not* sign it.
The same someone tore
the invitation into pieces
and left one piece
on my doorstep
and put one piece in the tree
and pasted one piece
on the paper ocean.
Someone did not think that

I, Nate the Great, could find out
who the someone was.
Someone was testing me.
I looked at the paper boat
on the paper water.
Hmmm. Paper and water.
I had just seen paper in water.
The phony clue in the sewer.
I, Nate the Great, had an idea.
Sludge and I ran home.
I filled my sink with water.
I took the two pieces
of the invitation
and turned them over
and put them in the water.
Now the printing on them

was wet and backward.

I, Nate the Great, looked
at the printing.

There was that funny E again.

The printing was the same
as the printing on the "phony clue."

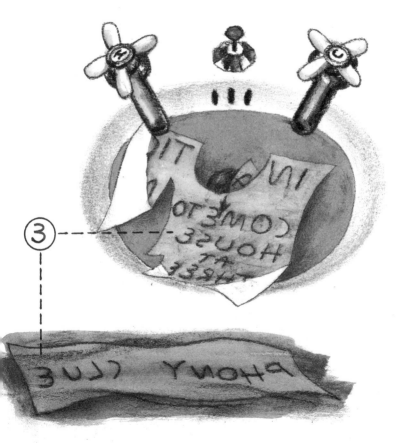

I, Nate the Great,

knew the case was solved.

It was not yet three o'clock.

This was an invitation

I wanted to answer exactly on time.

Sludge and I

ran around the block

and around the block

until it was three o'clock.

Then we went to Finley's house.

Finley was with Pip.

Pip did not say anything.

"It is three o'clock," I said.

"And I, Nate the Great, am here.

I have answered

your invitation, Finley."

Finley gulped.

"I, Nate the Great, say
there is no such thing
as a phony clue.
The printing on your phony clue
is the same as the printing
on the invitation.
You wrote the invitation.
You tore it into pieces."

Finley gulped again.

Pip opened his mouth.

At last he had
something to say.

"I win!" he said. "I told
Finley that you would
solve the case

by three o'clock."

"I lose," Finley said.

"You *are* a great detective."

"Thank you," I said.

I, Nate the Great, felt great.

I was glad the case was over.

Sludge and I started to run.

We ran past Annie and Fang.

"I solved the case!" I said.

"I knew you would!" Annie said.
Annie and Fang started to run
beside us.

We all ran home
for pancakes
and bones.

What's Inside

Ripped paper.
Paper shaped like boats.
Paper with secret messages.
Detectives deal with a lot of paper.
Nate studied up.

NATE'S NOTES: Paper

About 2,000 years ago, a man who was working for the Chinese emperor made the world's first paper. He created it from old rags and fishing nets.

In 1391, the Chinese emperor became the first person to use toilet paper. The paper was made just for him. Each sheet was about the size of a small towel.

4

In the year 1690, William Rittenhouse opened the first paper mill in North America. His paper factory was near Philadelphia. He made paper from rags. They were boiled, rinsed, and smashed into goo. The dried goo became paper.

In 1775, a man named Stephen Crane began selling paper to Paul Revere. Revere used the paper to print money. It was some of the first paper money ever printed in America. Crane's company still makes the paper for dollar bills. Paul Revere became famous for his midnight ride.

Today, most paper is made from bits of wood. The bits are called fiber. A French scientist got the idea while watching wasps build their nests.

Important Paper Products

1890—toilet paper on a roll

1907—paper towels

1924—paper tissues

1968—paper diapers

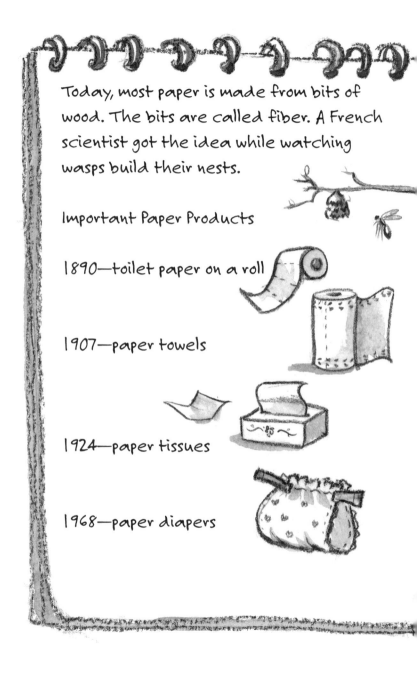

Many things we use every day are made from recycled (reused) paper fiber. Like what? Like cereal boxes, newspaper, notebook paper, and cardboard containers.

More than 50 percent of the paper used in the United States is collected for recycling. That works out to 342 pounds for every person in the country. That means that each person recycles paper weighing about as much as two adult men.

NATE'S NOTES: Ink

Ink goes with paper the way Sludge goes with Nate. They work best together. So Nate studied up on ink, too.

Before ink was invented, people wrote messages by carving pictures and letters into stone or pressing them into wet clay.

Thousands of years ago, the ancient Greeks invented the stylus. It was a tool made of bone, metal, or ivory. The Greeks used it to scratch marks into wooden tablets coated with wax.

About 5,000 years ago, the Chinese began using ink for writing. Their recipe? Soot, oil, and gelatin. Other people made ink from berries, plants, or rocks. The ink came in different colors, including black, blue, and red.

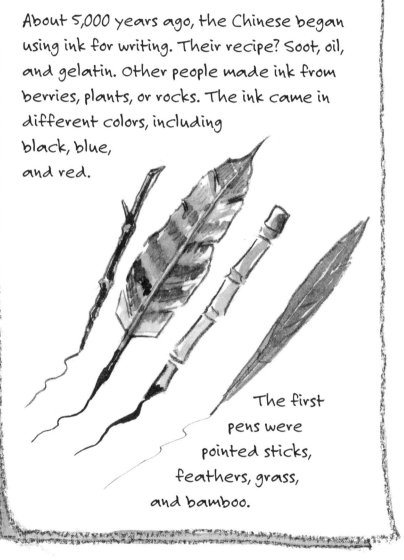

The first pens were pointed sticks, feathers, grass, and bamboo.

Lewis Waterman invented the fountain pen in 1884. Fountain pens worked much better than earlier pens. With a fountain pen, you don't have to keep dipping your pen in ink. Dipping can get messy—especially when the ink spills. Fountain pens have a small chamber inside to hold ink. One problem? Fountain pens often leak, blotch, or rip paper. Later pens, like the ballpoint and felt-tip, worked even better.

American chemist Thomas Sterry Hunt
created a special green ink in 1857. It's
hard to destroy and can't be easily
photographed. It's used to print American
money. That's why some people call dollars
greenbacks.

How to Make a Phony Log Cake

Looks like a log. Tastes like a cake. It's a cake in disguise.

Ask an adult to help you with this recipe.

GET TOGETHER:

- one pint of cold whipping cream
- a mixing bowl
- an electric mixer
- $1/2$ cup of powdered sugar
- 1 teaspoon of vanilla extract
- one package of round wafer cookies
- a spreading knife

- a large plate
- a fork
- $\frac{1}{4}$ cup of sweetened cocoa powder (like Nestlé's Quik)
- a sifter
- about 12 Hershey's Kisses
- about 12 mini-marshmallows
- 1 tablespoon of creamy peanut butter or Nutella or Marshmallow Fluff

MAKE YOUR PHONY LOG CAKE:

STEP ONE: *Make the Whipped Cream.*

1. Pour the whipping cream into the bowl.
2. Turn the mixer on to medium.
   Beat the cream until it is stiff.
   This should take
   about two minutes.*

3. Turn the electric mixer down to low.
   Mix the sugar and vanilla into the cream.

Here's how to tell whether the whipped cream is done.

- *Turn off the mixer.*
- *Pull the beaters up out of the cream. The cream should make little peaks where the beaters come out.*

STEP TWO: *Put Together Your Log.*

1. Using the knife, cover one side of a cookie with whipped cream.
2. Stack another cookie on top. Cover the second cookie with whipped cream. Add another cookie.
3. Keep stacking cookies and whipped cream until you have a tower of about twenty cookies. At some point the tower will become wobbly. Set it down on its side on the plate. Now it's a log.
4. Cover your log in a layer of whipped cream so that you can't see any of the cookies.

STEP THREE: *Complete the Disguise.*

1. Run the fork over the whipped cream. This will make the whipped cream look more like tree bark.

2. Sift the cocoa over the log. It's okay if some goes on the plate.

3. Make some phony mushrooms. Unwrap the Kisses. Put a Kiss (phony mushroom cap) on top of a mini-marshmallow (phony mushroom stem). Use a little peanut butter, Nutella, or Marshmallow Fluff to glue the pieces together and glue the mushrooms to the plate.

STEP FOUR: *Eat!*

Funny Pages

Q: What starts with a *t*, ends with a *t*, and is full of t?
A: *A teapot!*

Q: What three-letter word starts with gas?
A: *A car!*

Q: How do you make a witch itch?
A: *Take away the* w!

Q: What does the letter A have in common with a flower?
A: *They both have bees after them!*

Q: Take away my first letter. Take away my second letter. Take away all my letters and I stay the same. What am I?
A: *A letter carrier!*

Q: What word has only three letters but is longer than Nate?
A: *Banana!*

Q: What letter is always surprised?
A: G!

Q: What letter is always wet?
A: C!

Q: What two letters are always jealous?
A: N.V.

Q: What did A and B get in the record store?
A: A CD!

Q: What has four eyes but can't see?
A: Mississippi!

Q: Why is the letter G scary?
A: Because it turns host into ghost.

How to Send Secret Messages

Finley and Pip aren't the only ones who can send mysterious messages. You can, too. All you need is some invisible ink.

Ask an adult to help you.

GET TOGETHER:

- 2 tablespoons of baking soda
- 1 cup of water
- a cup
- a spoon
- a paintbrush
- white paper
- purple grape juice

WRITE YOUR MESSAGE:

1. Mix the baking soda and water in the cup.
2. Use the paintbrush to paint a message on the paper. The baking soda mixture is your ink.
3. Let the paper dry completely. Leave it overnight if possible. Your message should be invisible on the dry paper. Dust it off if you need to.
4. Reveal your message: Paint over the entire paper with grape juice. Be careful! Grape juice can stain.

How to Make Paper

Do you like to get messy? Then visit your family's recycling bin and turn some garbage into paper. It's not easy! But it's fun.

Ask an adult to help you.

GET TOGETHER:

- an apron, smock, or old shirt
- about a dozen pieces of scrap paper torn into small pieces (Try paper towels, construction paper, or tissue paper.)
- 2 dish tubs (One should be big enough so that you can lay the embroidery hoop flat inside.)
- water
- a piece of cheesecloth

- an embroidery hoop
- scissors
- a blender
- add-ins—like flower petals, tiny bits of tinsel, thread, or glitter
- a mixing spoon
- a sponge
- old towels

MAKE YOUR PAPER:

1. Put on your apron, smock, or old shirt. Choose a good place to work. A bathroom, kitchen, or backyard is best. You want someplace that can get wet.
2. Put the paper scraps in one of the tubs. Cover with water. Allow the paper to soak for at least an hour. Leave overnight if possible.

3. While the paper is soaking, make your frame. Stretch the cheesecloth tight inside the embroidery hoop. Use the scissors to trim the cheesecloth.

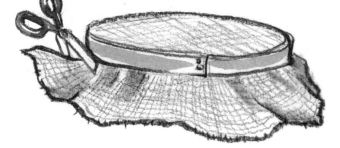

4. Fill the blender halfway
   with warm water.
   Add a handful
   of soaked paper.
   Blend until all the
   pieces are mixed in.

5. Pour the blended mixture into the second
   tub. Fill the tub halfway with warm water.
   Put in any add-ins you want to use. Mix
   thoroughly with the spoon.

6. Slide the embroidery hoop into the tub. Hold the hoop underwater. Gently move it back and forth to collect an even layer of pulp on the cheesecloth.

7. Lift the hoop out of the water. Hold it flat. Let it drip. Use the sponge to dry it off.

8. Place the old towels on a flat surface. Flip the hoop over on top of the towels. Gently lift off the hoop. The wet paper pulp should now be sitting on the towel.

9. Clean up your mess. Throw the soaked paper scraps back in the recycling bin. Scrub the blender.
10. Allow the pulp to dry for about one day. Put it outside in the sun. Or choose a warm place inside.
11. When the paper is dry, gently pull it off the towel.

12. Draw on your paper. Or give it as a gift.

More Funny Pages

Q: Why did the clock get sick?
A: *It was run down.*

Q: What's invisible and smells like carrots?
A: *Bunny farts!*

Q: How do you communicate with a fish?
A: *Drop him a line!*

Q: Why did the boy eat his homework?
A: *Because his teacher said it was a piece of cake.*

Q: What kind of dog tells time?
A: *A watch dog.*

Have you helped solve all
Nate the Great's mysteries?

❑ **Nate the Great**: Meet Nate, the great detective, and join him as he uses incredible sleuthing skills to solve his first big case.

❑ **Nate the Great Goes Undercover**: Who—or what—is raiding Oliver's trash every night? Nate bravely hides out in his friend's garbage can to catch the smelly crook.

❑ **Nate the Great and the Lost List**: Nate loves pancakes, but who ever heard of cats eating them? Is a strange recipe at the heart of this mystery?

❑ **Nate the Great and the Phony Clue**: Against ferocious cats, hostile adversaries, and a sly phony clue, Nate struggles to prove that he's still the world's greatest detective.

❑ **Nate the Great and the Sticky Case**: Nate is stuck with his stickiest case yet as he hunts for his friend Claude's valuable stegosaurus stamp.

❑ **Nate the Great and the Missing Key**: Nate isn't afraid to look anywhere—even under the nose of his friend's ferocious dog, Fang—to solve the case of the missing key.

❑ **Nate the Great and the Snowy Trail**: Nate has his work cut out for him when his friend Rosamond loses the birthday present she was going to give him. How can he find the present when Rosamond won't even tell him what it is?

❑ **Nate the Great and the Fishy Prize**: The trophy for the Smartest Pet Contest has disappeared! Will Sludge, Nate's clue-sniffing dog, help solve the case and prove he's worthy of the prize?

❑ **Nate the Great Stalks Stupidweed**: When his friend Oliver loses his special plant, Nate searches high and low. Who knew a little weed could be so tricky?

❑ **Nate the Great and the Boring Beach Bag**: It's no relaxing day at the beach for Nate and his trusty dog, Sludge, as they search through sand and surf for signs of a missing beach bag.

❑ **Nate the Great Goes Down in the Dumps**: Nate discovers that the only way to clean up this case is to visit the town dump. Detective work can sure get dirty!

❑ **Nate the Great and the Halloween Hunt**: It's Halloween, but Nate isn't trick-or-treating for candy. Can any of the witches, pirates, and robots he meets help him find a missing cat?

❑ **Nate the Great and the Musical Note**: Nate is used to looking for clues, not listening for them! When he gets caught in the middle of a musical riddle, can he hear his way out?

❑ **Nate the Great and the Monster Mess**: Nate loves his mother's deliciously spooky Monster Cookies, but the recipe has vanished! This is one case Nate and his growling stomach can't afford to lose.

❑ **Nate the Great, San Francisco Detective**: Nate visits his cousin Olivia Sharp in the big city, but it's no vacation. Can he find a lost joke book in time to save the world?

❑ **Nate the Great and the Big Sniff**: Nate depends on his dog, Sludge, to help him solve all his cases. But Nate is on his own this time, because Sludge has disappeared! Can Nate solve the case and recover his canine buddy?

❑ **Nate the Great on the Owl Express**: Nate boards a train to guard Hoot, his cousin Olivia Sharp's pet owl. Then Hoot vanishes! Can Nate find out *whooo* took the feathered creature?